SALMA

Makes a Home

Story by
**Danny
Ramadan**

Art by
**Anna
Bron**

**annick
press**
toronto • berkeley

Cover art by Anna Bron, designed by Sara Loos based on art direction by Paul Covello
Interior designed by Sara Loos and Paul Covello

Edited by Claire Caldwell
Copy edited by Erin Chan
Proofread by Eleanor Gasparik

Annick Press Ltd.

We acknowledge the support of the Canada Council for the Arts and
the Ontario Arts Council, and the participation of the Government of Canada/
la participation du gouvernement du Canada for our publishing activities.

ONTARIO ARTS COUNCIL
CONSEIL DES ARTS DE L'ONTARIO
an Ontario government agency
un organisme du gouvernement de l'Ontario

Library and Archives Canada Cataloguing in Publication

Title: Salma makes a home / story by Danny Ramadan ; art by Anna Bron.
Names: Ramadan, Ahmad Danny, author. | Bron, Anna, 1989- illustrator.
Identifiers: Canadiana (print) 20220412898 | Canadiana (ebook) 2022041291X | ISBN 9781773217611
   (hardcover) | ISBN 9781773217628 (softcover) | ISBN 9781773217642 (PDF) | ISBN 9781773217635
   (HTML)
Classification: LCC PS8635.A4613 S23 2023 | DDC jC813/.6,Äîdc23

Published in the U.S.A. by Annick Press (U.S.) Ltd.
Distributed in Canada by University of Toronto Press.
Distributed in the U.S.A. by Publishers Group West.

Printed in Canada

annickpress.com
dannyramadan.com
annabron.com

Also available as an e-book. Please visit annickpress.com/ebooks for more details.

Table of Contents

Chapter 1

With her little scissors, Salma carefully snips off a final thread then looks at her beautiful handiwork: a colorful paper lantern she learned how to make online.

"Mama, look. I made this to celebrate the arrival of Ramadan." She used red papers and drew little geometric designs along its edges. "Red for the Canadian flag, and mosaic like the mosques of Damascus."

Mama lifts up the lantern and smiles, examining it in the living room light. "What a wonderful piece of art, Salma. A great way to celebrate the arrival of our holy month."

"I based it on my own memories," Salma says. She remembers seeing al-mesaher walking the alleyways of Damascus right before sunrise. His son walked beside him sleepily, holding a real lantern in his hand to light the way. Al-mesaher knocked on a little drum to wake people up to eat their suhour: the pre-fasting meal.

"Do you think al-mesaher will come to visit us in Vancouver, Mama?" Salma asks.

Mama returns the paper lantern to Salma. "Maybe when your Baba comes here, he will be your personal mesaher."

Knock, knock knock knock, knock. Mama taps her knuckles on the coffee table then sings, "Wake up and eat suhour, let Ramadan visit you."

Salma giggles.

"Now off to bed, young lady," Mama says. "You have school tomorrow."

In bed, Salma closes her eyes and wishes for Baba to come here soon. Vancouver has been a beautiful new home: Salma loves the seawall and its many seagulls. She learned how to skate at the ice rink, and she looks great in her purple rain jacket. But there is something missing that she can't figure out. Is it how much she misses Baba? Is it how different this city is from her hometown back in Syria? She isn't sure.

In her dreams, Salma walks the streets of

Damascus with Baba. He wears a red fez on his head and a long silky shawl on his shoulders.

"Let's go celebrate Ramadan's return together, Salma," Baba says. He holds his little drum by his chest and knocks on it.

Knock, knock knock knock, knock.

Salma looks around. This is her old school in Damascus, and that's her favorite candy store. Over there is the little park where she used to climb the slide from the slippery side. At the end of the road is her old home.

Suddenly, as if they were made of clouds, the buildings blur then disappear. One after another, the buildings turn to smoke, and in a moment, they are gone. Salma's heart aches. She feels a burn in her eyes.

"Baba, why is this happening?" Salma presses herself closer to Baba and squeezes his hand.

"Because you've forgotten what they look like, Salma," Baba says. He pulls his fingers away from hers and walks away. He waves goodbye then knocks on his little drum.

Knock, knock knock knock, knock.

"Baba, please don't leave me again." Salma feels her heart fluttering like a bird trying to escape a cage. She runs after Baba, but her feet are heavy. The streets around her blur, and her little home in

Damascus turns to smoke. She is scared. "Baba, come back."

Knock, knock knock knock, knock.

Chapter 2

Salma opens her eyes, startled. That was a scary dream. She hears the knocking once more, as if it echoes back from her nightmare. Then she realizes it's just Mama, knocking on her bedroom door.

"Is it morning yet?" Salma rubs her eyes as Mama comes into her room.

"I have such good news for you, Salma," Mama says. Mama's news makes Salma leap out of bed.

She and Mama dance around the room before Salma has to get ready for school.

Salma races out of the apartment. Her best friend, Riya, runs to catch up.

"Salma, wait!" Riya says. "Why are we running?"

"I have such good news that I want to share with everyone!"

Salma rushes into her classroom and almost crashes into Ms. Singh's chair. "Baba finally got his papers sorted," Salma announces in front of the whole class. "He will join us in Canada soon!"

Riya squeezes Salma's hands, a big smile on her face. "I'm so happy for you, Salma!"

"You have been waiting for so long," Ayman says from the back of the classroom.

The other students cheer for Salma. Her heart beats so fast; it feels as if it's going to jump out of her chest. She thanks everyone and squeezes Riya's hands back.

"Why don't you tell us about your father?" Ms. Singh asks.

Salma shares one of her favorite memories: the time Baba built them a swing on their balcony back in Damascus. At first, she was scared because the swing went too high. "But then, I grew up, and I wasn't scared anymore," Salma says.

She tells them about the yummy sandwiches he

used to make her: he warmed the bread and melted the cheese first, then added a layer of strawberry jam on top.

"Mama makes really good sandwiches," Salma adds, "but they are not like Baba's."

"When was the last time you saw your Baba?" Ms. Singh asks.

"A year, eleven months, and six days ago," Salma says. "We were standing outside our old home in Damascus, and I asked Baba if we could just take the house with us."

"The whole house?" Ms. Singh asks. "That's a funny thought!"

"I just wanted to hide Baba in the house and bring him," Salma says. She doesn't know why, but she feels as if a fire burns behind her eyes. Her bad dream flashes in her mind. "It was the day we left Baba behind in Syria."

"What did your house look like back in Damascus, Salma?" Natalie asks. "I've never been outside of Canada."

"It had two bedrooms," Salma says confidently. "No. Three? It was a three-bedroom home." Salma suddenly feels unsure. What was the color of the walls in the living room? How many pillows did she have on her bed? What fabric were the curtains of her bedroom window? She can't remember.

Salma feels small. She crosses her arms over her chest and looks at the ground. Tears gather in her eyes. Salma doesn't understand why she is sad. It's a happy day. Baba will be here soon, and he will love everything about Canada. She shouldn't feel sad.

She sniffs then makes herself smile. "I'm just so happy he's coming," Salma says. Her voice quivers.

"It's okay to be sad that Baba is not around, Salma," Ms. Singh cuts in before other students ask more questions. "Sometimes, we get sad in our hearts, but we know in our heads we will be happy when we see our loved ones again."

"I'm not sad," Salma insists, quiet at first, then louder as she continues. "Baba will be here soon, and he will love it here."

But what if he doesn't? The thought rushes through Salma's mind. Quiet at first, then louder, too. Soon, it is the only thing Salma can think about.

Chapter 3

On her way home from school, Salma can't think of anything to talk about with Riya, like they usually do. She watches her steps so she doesn't step in a puddle and silently gazes at the trees. Salma sees an empty bird's nest on a branch.

"Are you mad at me, Salma?" Riya asks.

"No. No. Just thinking," Salma says. "Do you think that's a swallow's nest?"

"What's a swallow?" Riya is confused.

"It's a small blue bird with a red head and white wings." Salma is surprised that Riya doesn't know her favorite bird.

"I've never seen one!" Riya says. "Are you sure you didn't dream them?"

"They are everywhere in Damascus," Salma mumbles. "Or at least I think so?" The burning in her eyes returns. Salma stops walking. She tightens her hand around her umbrella.

Riya looks back at Salma. "What's wrong?" she asks.

"I don't know. I'm really happy that Baba is coming but . . ." Salma pauses then confesses, "I feel scared, too."

Riya takes Salma's hand and steps closer to her. Their umbrellas smack against each other. Riya's caring eyes make Salma feel warm inside. "Why are you scared?" Riya asks.

"I'm worried that Baba won't like this new home," Salma says. She feels the burn in her eyes again. She sniffles. "What if he hates the straight roads and prefers Damascus's old alleyways? What if he dislikes the tall buildings and misses our small home? What

if he misses my grandparents, the way that I miss him?"

Riya's eyes tear up, too. She tightens her hand on Salma's. Salma feels the warmth of her best friend's fingers, even though both of their hands are cold. "Salma, when my family came here, I didn't like it either," Riya says. "I didn't like the new language I had to learn and didn't enjoy the cold, rainy winters."

"You didn't?" Salma is surprised. Riya is the smartest kid in their grade. She always reads in front of the whole class. She has an accent, just like Salma, but Ms. Singh, their teacher, also has an accent. And when it snowed last February, Riya and Salma played in the snow together for hours. They even built a snowman.

"The language was hard, but I learned it. The winters are cold, but I love my colorful gloves and my soft scarf," Riya says. "Now I love Vancouver, and your Baba will, too."

But what if he doesn't? Salma feels the burning behind her eyes again. But maybe Riya is right. Maybe all it will take for Baba to love Vancouver is good language practice and some warm clothes. She takes a deep breath and nods at her best friend. They walk home holding hands the whole way.

Chapter 4

"WELCOME HOME!" Salma's banner says, once in English and again in Arabic. The airport's automatic glass doors slide open, and Salma raises her banner higher. The red and white balloons that Salma and Mama tied to a park bench bounce in the spring air and glimmer under the warm sun. But Baba doesn't come through the doors. Salma sighs and lowers the banner.

"He will be here soon," Riya reassures her. She came with her Maa to support Salma and Mama. "He is probably finishing his immigration papers."

"I can keep an eye on the gates for you, Salma." Ayman came to support them, too. He holds a large flower arrangement his father brought.

"You don't know what my Baba looks like," Salma insists.

A car parks in front of them, blocking their view. Salma wishes the people in the car would hurry up so she can keep her eyes out for Baba. The car doors open, and a small family steps out. A father, a mother, and two children.

"We'll miss you," the father says.

"Call us all the time," the girl says.

The mother opens the trunk, and the father helps

her pull out two large suitcases. She hugs her husband then leans down to squeeze her children close. "I will miss you, too," the mother says. "But you know I have to go."

The boy hugs his mother one last time. The girl nods then buries her face into her father's side while her mother crosses the road, waves a final goodbye, and then disappears into the airport.

"She will be gone for so long," the girl says. Salma sees tears on her face.

"You promised your mom not to cry." The father pats her head as he opens the car door.

Salma's hands feel weak. She lowers her sign again. She feels the burn return to her eyes. Salma promised Baba she wouldn't cry when she said goodbye to him, too. *No crying today*, Salma reminds herself. *Today is a happy day.* She shakes her head and sniffles.

"Are you okay, Salma?" Mama asks. She tries to hug her, but Salma escapes the hug, nods quickly, and raises the sign even higher than before.

At the airport doors, a familiar figure appears.

"It's Baba!" Salma shouts.

Mama looks up. Salma sees a tear sliding down her cheek. Baba waves at them, a huge smile on his face. Finally, he crosses the street, drops his luggage, and kneels down to give Salma a big hug. She dips her face into his shoulder and smells his familiar cologne.

"I missed you so much, Baba," Salma says in English.

"Huh?" Baba looks confused.

"I missed you so much!" she repeats in Arabic, and he nods, taking Mama's hand. "Baba, these are my friends and their families." Salma introduces everyone to Baba in Syrian Arabic.

"I hope the trip wasn't too hard on you," Ayman's father says in Egyptian Arabic. Salma understands

Egyptian Arabic, even when Egyptians pronounce the letter G in a funny way.

"It wasn't too bad." Baba's face lights up. "I'm happy to be with my family."

Riya's Maa offers to drive on the way home, and Salma sits next to her Baba in the backseat.

"How are you?" Baba asks Maa with his limited English.

"I am good," Riya's Maa says slowly to make sure Baba understands.

Salma wiggles in her middle seat. Baba is finally here. Canada is now his home. She has to make him love everything about it, or else he might go back to Syria.

"Baba, this is the Fraser River." She points out the window. "You will love walking across the bridges on it. And that's a park where people play tennis. Do you want to play tennis? That's the road that takes you to Granville Island, where they have yummy grilled potatoes and funny hats. This is the ocean! Look at how big it is, and all the ships! Baba, you will love all of these things in no time."

Baba looks back at Salma with confusion in his eyes, and Mama places a quick hand on her knee. "It's very exciting that Baba is here, Salma," Mama says. "We have all the time in the world to show him all of these new things."

Salma pouts: if they wait too long, Baba won't fall in love with Vancouver, and he might not want to stay. She has to make sure he enjoys this city as soon as possible.

"Baba, we will all go out and talk English to everyone," Salma says. "You'll try poutine, and we can go snowshoeing, too."

"Salma, let Baba rest!" Mama insists.

Riya's Maa pulls up outside their building. "You must be excited to show Baba your home, Salma," Riya says. "I loved it when I visited last time."

Salma smiles at Riya. *That's a brilliant idea! Baba will love our home here,* Salma thinks. *This will be the first step for him to love Vancouver, too.*

Chapter 5

When they get to their apartment, Baba walks through the door with his right foot first.

"What's Baba doing, Mama?" Salma asks.

"It's for good luck." Mama looks surprised. "It's a Syrian tradition, Salma. Don't you remember?"

Salma nods, but the truth is that she didn't remember until Mama explained.

Baba slowly takes in the details of the home. The paintings that Mama got for cheap at an antique store; the large TV that a neighbor donated to them; the books Salma collects and organizes on her bookshelf; Salma's drawings hanging on the silver fridge; and the blue and gold rocking chair.

"These are so beautiful, Salma," Baba says, pointing to her drawings. He opens his arms to Salma, and she runs in, hugging him quickly.

"Baba, promise not to leave us alone again," Salma whispers. The burn in her eyes returns.

"What?" Baba says. "Why would you think I would, Salma?"

"Never mind," Salma says quickly. She sniffles then twirls a bit. "Mama makes us our clothes now. She made me this dress."

Baba frowns. He eyes Mama, who nods, and then looks back at Salma. "It's a very pretty dress," Baba says.

While Mama makes dinner, Baba and Salma unpack his suitcase. Between his clothes and shoes, Salma finds a jar filled with jasmine flowers.

"It's from the jasmine tree outside our old home," Baba tells her. "I brought it with me to remember." Salma twists open the lid and takes a big inhale; the jasmine smell takes her back to the day Mama taught her how to make jasmine necklaces and bracelets, then made the two of them jasmine tea.

"Do you miss Damascus, Salma?" Baba asks. Salma pauses and buries her nose in the jar.

Sometimes, Salma does miss Damascus. She misses the funny conversations Baba and Jiddo had when they played backgammon. She misses the cold ceramic floors in her favorite mosque. She misses the tastes of her Tita's many yummy homemade desserts.

"Not really," Salma lies. If she tells Baba how she feels, it might remind him of how much he loves their home back there. It's better to have only one home: only here. But she can't help asking, "Will *you* miss it, Baba?"

"Oh, Salma, of course I will," Baba says while unwrapping a beautiful backgammon set. "It's our homeland and birthplace. It's very meaningful to me. I already miss Syria a lot."

Salma's feet feel cold. *Will Baba go back, then? What if he doesn't like it here at all?* She takes a deep breath and keeps her thoughts to herself.

Baba opens a box of Syrian sweets and offers one to Salma. "Here is a little reminder of our beautiful Syria," he says. "Those I brought from my own Baba's shop. Your Jiddo!"

Salma pops the dessert in her mouth, letting it melt slowly on her tongue like a snowflake she caught on a snowy day. Baba pulls out a smooth piece of silk he brought for Mama. When Salma touches it, it reminds her of her Tita's beautiful praying shawl. It makes her miss her grandmother, too.

"This is the last thing," Baba says. He opens a family album he brought with him, which Salma and Mama forgot to pack when they left. His many documents are hidden inside: his university diploma and letters from his bosses in Damascus. "Let's see where we can store all of this," Baba says to Salma, and Salma follows. She thinks maybe she should hide all of these things somewhere Baba will never see them so he won't remember Damascus. She doesn't want anything from Damascus anymore; not even the sweets.

That night, way past her bedtime, Salma is still awake. She tosses and turns in her comfy bed. She sighs and holds the pillow over her head. She feels the burn in her eyes again.

What is this? she wonders. *I should be happy that Baba is here. But why am I scared? Why do I feel like something bad is about to happen?*

Salma cannot sleep with all of these thoughts in her head. She quietly steps out of her room and walks to the kitchen for a glass of water. She then tiptoes up to her parents' half-opened bedroom door. In the night-light shadows, she sees both Mama and Baba sleeping in bed.

I just . . . I just don't want him to leave us again, she thinks. Tears flow down her cheeks. She quickly dries them with her pajama sleeves, goes back to her bedroom, and closes the door behind her. "No. We have to make him love this new place. We have to," she whispers to herself and buries her head in her pillow.

Chapter 6

English is hard, but Baba is trying his best.

Since Baba arrived, Salma has been helping him with homework from his language classes. She's taught him how to say hello and to say that he likes a meal Mama made.

"I don't know how you learned so fast," Baba tells Salma on a Saturday morning. She drags Baba back to the dining room table, while Mama cleans after breakfast, and opens his language books and notebooks.

"You just have to repeat the word in your head ten times. Then it will stay there," Salma tells him. "Let's try again. Repeat after me: Delicious."

"De-less-yous," Baba tries.

"No, Baba. It's 'delicious.' These stuffed zucchinis are delicious."

"But where did the *shhhh* sound come from?" Baba is confused.

Salma shrugs. "Just give it one more try!"

"I'm tired, Salma," Baba complains. "It's Saturday. Let's take a day off."

Salma gives up. Baba closes his notebook and stretches. "I want to watch a Syrian soap opera."

"What if you watched a local TV show?" Salma asks. "You will learn new words."

"I just want to hear our own language for a bit, Salma," Baba insists.

Salma's heart sinks as Baba grabs the remote and switches the channel to a Syrian show. What if the show reminds him how much he misses Syria?

He points out the background in the scene to Salma. It's a beautiful garden in the heart of Damascus.

"Remember when we went there for a picnic?" he asks. "Ahh. How I miss these beautiful places."

Salma crosses her arms on her chest and squeezes hard. She fights the urge to turn off the television and run crying to her room. She sits silently watching Baba as he watches TV, laughing at the funny jokes in Arabic. He clearly misses Arabic and prefers it to English. What if he goes back to Syria so he can speak Arabic to everyone he knows? She spent weeks and months missing him while he was there and she was here. Sometimes, she almost cried when she talked to him on the phone, even when she promised she wouldn't. She doesn't want to feel this way again: no more long-distance phone calls, no more nights watching Mama work hard alone, no more days when the only way for her to see him is on a phone screen.

And it's not just English that's a problem for Baba! She also overheard Baba and Mama talking. He can't find a job like he had back in Syria. Salma remembers how much he loved his job as an accountant: his little office and his prized laptop. He enjoyed working with numbers and charts. The only job he's been able to get in Canada is at a construction site, building new homes down the street from where they live. On his workdays, he comes home tired. He showers and quickly goes to bed. Salma barely has any time to show him all the things she loves about Canada.

"How about we go for a walk on the seawall?" Salma says. She turns off the TV. "It's my favorite place in all of Vancouver." Maybe that will make Baba want to stay!

"That's a great idea for a sunny spring day," Mama

says from the kitchen. Salma grabs Baba's jacket, and she stands on the sofa to help him put it on.

As they walk, Salma can't take her eyes off of Baba. She watches him take in the beautiful views and the mountains covered in snow. She sees him smile when Mama points out all the seagulls gathering on a rock in the ocean. Maybe this is it: he will love the seawall

so much, he will forget about the beautiful gardens in Damascus.

"This place is so far away from our old home," Baba whispers. The words stick in Salma's mind the way wet sand clings to her shoes. It's so frustrating that nothing she does is working to make Baba love it here.

"But it is beautiful in its own ways," Salma says. A gust of wind blows on them.

"Can we go home?" Baba finally says, looking at Mama. "I am cold." He walks toward the main road before Salma and Mama have a chance to change his mind.

"Watch out!"

They all hear the shout from behind. Mama grabs Baba's arm and manages to pull him away from the bike lane, which he stepped into by mistake.

"Watch where you're going!" the cyclist shouts at Baba in English.

"I am sorry. I don't understand what you are saying," Baba replies in Arabic.

"What kind of stupid language is that?" the cyclist shouts back. "Go back to where you came from!" he screams before pedaling away.

"See? No one understands our language here," Baba says. He sounds upset. "This place is so different from everything I know. What a challenge it will be to get used to it."

"That terrible cyclist had no right to speak to you that way," Mama says, "no matter what language you speak or how you look. You need time to adjust, but you should never change for people like that." She pulls at his hand, and they keep on walking.

Watching the cyclist disappear around a curve in the seawall, Salma feels the burn again behind her eyes. Baba hates it here. No matter what she does, she won't be able to keep him around. He's going to leave again.

She follows her Baba and Mama silently. Her brain replays the memories of her missing Baba, and the burn behind her eyes grows hotter.

Chapter 7

When Salma and her parents get home, Baba says he needs a nap and goes straight to the bedroom.

Salma sits on the floor in the living room, listening to the silence around her. When Baba leaves, it will be just her and Mama. She loves Mama, but she loves Baba, too. When he leaves, who will make her the best sandwiches with melted cheese? Who else would be strong enough to lift her up and twirl her around?

She knows she will miss Baba terribly, like she missed him before.

"Salma, are you okay?" Mama asks her. "You look upset."

"Baba's going to leave us and go back to Syria," Salma says, between clenched teeth.

"Salma, Baba will never leave us." Mama looks surprised. "What makes you think that?"

Salma feels the burn in her eyes once more. She can't cry, though. She made a promise not to. If Baba sees her cry, he will think she doesn't want him here. "Because he will miss Damascus more than he loves us," she says. "He doesn't smile the way he used to back in Syria. He doesn't chitchat with me before bed. He doesn't take his coffee on the balcony in the mornings either."

Mama takes a step back and silently examines Salma. Salma feels as if the house around her is getting darker. She feels as if the walls are squeezing her in. This house is not good enough for Baba to call it home. No matter how many beautiful decorations she adds or paintings she does, it won't be good enough to keep Baba here. Not when Baba is challenged with his English and struggling to find the job he wants. Not when people shout at him because he speaks Arabic—the language he loves. Not when everything is so different to him. This house will never be a home for him. The thought takes over Salma's whole body.

"Baba doesn't like this new home," Salma shouts at Mama.

"Salma, take a deep breath," Mama says. She holds out her arms, but Salma doesn't run into them like usual. Mama can't do anything to help her, not when Baba will leave again. Salma saw how tired Mama used to be before Baba joined them in Canada; she knows she will be too tired again without Baba. A hug from Mama won't help make Baba love this house.

"You hear him, don't you? He said it yesterday. He said that the ceiling is so low compared to our old home back in Damascus." She stretches her arms, as if to touch the ceiling. "He always covers his shoulders with this blanket because it's colder here compared to Damascus. He shivers, too. I saw it with my own eyes."

Mama comes closer then sits on the floor next to Salma. "Baba is allowed some time to adjust and get used to our new home. It's okay if he misses Damascus, too."

"I live here, and I don't miss Damascus at all," Salma says. "I don't even remember Damascus." Her eyes burn even more. It feels like her whole face is red like fire.

"I'm sure that's not true," Mama says.

"It is. I don't miss Damascus, not even a little. Not even at all!" Salma shouts. "Damascus is stupid. It wants to take Baba away from me."

"Salma!" Mama says sternly. "Don't say that. Damascus is your birthplace."

"I hate Damascus!" Salma runs into her bedroom. She slams the door.

Chapter 8

Salma hears a soft knock on her bedroom door.

"Hey, Salma," Baba says, "may I come in?"

Salma tightens the sheets around her and squeezes her fairy doll closer. She feels the weight of Baba as he sits on the edge of her mattress. He strokes her hair.

"Hey, I made you a cheese sandwich," Baba says. "With strawberry jam."

He holds out a dish with her favorite sandwich on it. She takes a bite. The melted cheese, warm and soft like caramel, feels good in her mouth.

"I heard you had a conversation with Mama," Baba says softly.

"You don't love it here," Salma says. "I think you want to go back to Syria."

Baba sighs then leans against the headboard. "It's not that I don't like it here, Salma. I just miss Damascus."

"Why? This home is beautiful and new. We have a dishwasher and a beautiful balcony. We even have a little swing in the park," Salma says.

"Yes. We have all of these things, and they are beautiful. But I need other things, too."

"Exactly! And if you can't get those other things here, you'll leave us." Salma feels the burn in her eyes again. "When you were away, I missed you so much. I missed your smile and the way you hold my hand. I missed your jokes and your pranks."

This time, Salma lets her tears flow. She cries such big tears that they drop onto the plate. Her tears are hot like the lava of a volcano. Her throat now burns, too, and so do her ears. Baba puts the dish on Salma's bedside table then squeezes her in his arms.

"I missed you, too, Salma," Baba says. "I missed the smell of your hair, and your giggle, and the way you fell asleep in my arms while watching TV. Why do you think I worked so hard to join you here?"

"You did?" Salma says between her tears.

"Of course. We had to leave Syria and come here for a better life," Baba says. "It took a lot of work to find a way here, and it was very sad to see you and Mama go while I had to stay in Damascus. I was lonely, and I worried about you a lot. Now that I am here, I would never leave you two again. No matter how hard it is."

"Even when it's cold?" Salma sniffles. "You won't leave us for stupid Damascus?"

"I promise I will never ever leave you, Salma." Baba has a smile on his face: an understanding one, like the one he has whenever Salma stumbles on a difficult math problem. Salma buries her face in her Baba's chest again.

"Remember Damascus, Salma?" Baba says. "Remember that evening you and Mama came with me to an old café?"

"When you played backgammon with Jiddo?" Salma lifts her head up. She does remember when her parents took her to that historical café. The beautiful alleyways zigzagged like a maze, yellow and orange lanterns hanging from their walls.

"Yes. You listened to al-hakawati telling beautiful stories on the stage. Remember that?" Baba asks.

Salma nods. She remembers the old man with a large handwritten book filled with stories from Syrian history and from his own imagination. She remembers the taste of jasmine tea and the yummy cheese bread they got after.

They also visited the Ummayad Mosque that day. She adored running barefoot there, while her parents sat down for a quick prayer after the lovely evening they spent in the café.

"Do you remember how cozy our home in Damascus was?" Baba asks.

"You had to work extra time to be able to afford it," Salma says, feeling the tears returning.

"But you didn't think Damascus was stupid then, did you?" Baba asks gently.

"No," Salma admits. "I loved it there."

"Damascus is worthy of your love—it was the place you grew up in."

"Baba . . ." Salma struggles to put words to what she feels. "I am starting to forget some stuff about Syria."

"Does that scare you?" Baba asks, stroking her hair once more. Salma nods and bites her lower lip. Baba squeezes her in closer. "It's okay, my child. What matters is that you remember the important stuff. The good stuff. That you remember the people you love and the traditions that mean a lot to you. That you remember your language, even if you don't use it every day. You remember the smell of our food and the joy of our gatherings." Baba offers the half-eaten sandwich to Salma again.

"Are you going to love Vancouver, then?"

"I am sure I will with time," Baba says, "but that's not something you need to worry about. It's not your job to make me love the city. Just like you, I will love it in my own time."

Baba puts his warm hand on her shoulder, and she smiles, feeling like a weight has been lifted off her.

"It's okay to have two homes, Salma," he says. "One that you live in, and one that lives within you."

Salma is not sure she understands, but she feels better now. Baba won't leave her for anything. She burrows her head into Baba's chest, and he hugs her closer. "You're my favorite human on the whole planet," Salma says.

"What about Mama?" Baba says. "You made her sad when you shouted at her. Maybe you need to apologize?"

"I will apologize." Salma nods. "Right after I finish this sandwich."

Chapter 9

Salma stands at the corner of her street, waiting for Riya. Finally, she sees her friend coming. Riya crosses the street and gives Salma a hug.

"How was your weekend?" Riya asks, and Salma tells her of the walks on the seawall with her parents and the English language homework she helped Baba with.

"His English is getting much better," Salma says,

"and in his free time, he's still applying for jobs as an accountant. He has a job interview today."

"It seems like your Baba is getting used to Canada, then," Riya says.

"Yes," Salma says, "I think he is starting to like it here."

The two friends walk together to school; the spring sun shines. Salma feels a wet dot on her forehead. It's a beautiful red leaf. She smiles while pink and purple blossoms rain down on them every time a gust of wind shakes the trees.

"But Baba said something I didn't understand, Riya," Salma says. "He said that it's okay to have two homes at the same time."

"I wonder what that means. Is he talking about Syria?"

"I'm not sure." Salma tries to remember the road she and her Baba took to school every day back in Damascus. Did they take a right turn, or a left? Did they pass by the bus loop? Maybe the old supermarket where they sell all kinds of cheese? "Do you miss India, Riya?" she asks her friend.

"I don't really remember it," Riya says. "I was only four when we left India for Pakistan. That was years before we came to Canada."

"So, you don't miss the place you were born?" Salma asks. "Do you think that's okay?"

"I think I miss it, just in a different way," Riya says.

Salma hesitates then admits, "I am starting to forget Damascus."

Riya stops walking. She squeezes Salma's hand. "I

don't know what to say. I'm sorry you feel this way, Salma."

The two friends walk in silence. Salma looks up at the trees and watches two birds chase each other across the branches. Riya watches the birds, too. One of them dives to the ground, picks up a twig, and flies back up to a small nest.

"Are these swallows?" Riya asks. "They look like the birds you told me about."

"No. I think these are sparrows," Salma says. "Ms. Singh let me borrow a book about birds in Canada. These look like sparrows."

"They are rebuilding their home," Riya says. "The wind last night must have knocked their nest down."

The school bell rings in the distance, and they rush toward the gate. On their way to their classroom, Riya says, "My Maa misses India. That I know for sure. She teaches me about it all the time."

Riya tells Salma of the many ways her Maa keeps reminders of India in their home: the beautiful orange flowers she hangs on a wall, the mosaic tables she only uses when important guests come to visit, and the many photos she has of the city they came from.

"Maa says that it's important to keep your birthplace alive in your heart," Riya says, "even if it's far away on the map."

"Maybe that's what Baba means," Salma says. "Maybe that's how you have two homes at the same time."

All through the school day, Salma can't think of anything other than her Baba's words, the two sparrows, and what Riya told her. *What are the important things worth remembering? What are the things she wants to keep from Syria? If they can't go back to Damascus, how can she bring Damascus here to Canada? Not only for her but also for Baba and Mama, too.*

By the time she gets home, Salma already has a plan.

Chapter 10

All the lights are on in Salma's home.

Mama climbs the ladder with a little piece of tape. Salma hands her another paper lantern with a small battery candlelight inside. Mama secures the hanging thread to the ceiling, flips the switch, and the lantern—green like the fields around Damascus—glimmers. All the other lanterns are lit.

Salma steps back and looks at all the different

lanterns she and her Mama made. They look like little Damascene homes floating in the air. Salma imagines them filled with people she knew: her Tita and Jiddo, her friends from back in Damascus, and all of her cousins.

"I'm back." Baba walks in the door. He carries large packages in his hands. "These lanterns look like stars and moons in the sky!"

Salma twirls a bit, proud of herself. Then she runs toward him and plants a kiss on his cheek. She takes one of the packages from his hands.

"It was easy to print these at the local drugstore," he says. "I even asked for the price in English!"

Excitedly, Salma unwraps it. Inside is a frame with a picture from their photo album, large and colorful. It's the three of them walking down an old alleyway near their home in Damascus. Salma is in the middle, hanging onto Baba's and Mama's hands, swinging her feet in the air.

"I love it!" Salma says. With Mama's help, Baba steps up on the sofa, hammers a nail into the wall, and

then uses a wire to hang the picture there. Meanwhile, Salma unwraps the other photo they picked: the Ummayad Mosque courtyard, with its ceramic floor glittering under a sunny sky filled with swallows. She helps Baba hang it in the hallway.

"I made us some jasmine tea." Mama offers Baba and Salma cups filled with the tea she made using the dried flowers Baba brought with him from their old home.

"It smells so good," Salma says, inhaling deeply. The three of them sit around, enjoying their tea. Salma smiles as she sees Baba and Mama cozying up to one another on the sofa. Even when Baba is cold, Mama is there with her warm hugs.

"Salma asked me to make you a surprise," Mama says.

"Mama! Not yet!" Salma insists.

"I think Baba will love his new gift," Mama says. She pulls a little bag from beside her sewing machine. She offers it to Baba, who opens it. He takes a beautiful silky shawl out. He *oohs* at the beautiful fabric and the perfect design.

"My own Baba has one just like it," he says, wrapping the shawl around his shoulders. "It's so soft and warm! Thank you," he says to Mama. "And thank you, Salma, for thinking of me."

The ringer goes off on Salma's tablet, just as she planned. She quickly answers the call. On its screen, Tita and Jiddo appear. They wave at Baba with big smiles, and Baba says hi to them.

Tita tells them of the latest feast they had with their relatives, and Jiddo shows them his own shawl, very similar to the one Mama made for Baba. Baba tells them of his new work in Vancouver and the hard time he is having learning English.

"You moved across the world for a better future," Jiddo says. "It's okay that you need some time to learn."

"You were always the smartest kid in school," Tita says.

"I miss you so much," Baba tells his parents in Arabic. "I miss you a lot," he repeats in English. Everyone laughs.

"See? You are already learning!" Tita says.

Chapter 11

That night, both Salma and Baba ask for seconds of the dinner that Mama prepared: a yummy mfarakeh with cauliflower, meat, lemon, and parsley, and a fatoush salad on the side.

"It's so delicious," Baba says in English, and they all laugh.

With another round of jasmine tea in their hands, the family is ready to settle down. "How about we play

a game?" Baba says. He pulls the backgammon set out and opens it up like a book.

"But I don't know how to play backgammon," Salma says.

"I will teach you how!"

Salma mixes her white pieces with Baba's black, and Baba laughs. Together, they set the pieces in their right spots. He teaches her how to throw the two dice so they hit the sides of the wooden backgammon board.

Knock, knock knock knock, knock.

The dice twirl for a moment before they settle on the numbers three and five. "These are good numbers," Baba says. "Now you have to move your pieces wisely."

Biting the tip of her tongue, Salma thinks of her

next steps and moves her pieces according to the number.

"See! You're a natural!" Baba announces. Salma, surrounded by the lights of her homey lanterns, the sounds of her family's laughter, the touch of the backgammon wood, and the taste of the jasmine tea on her tongue, finally feels at home.

When it's Salma's bedtime, Baba says he will tuck her in, and Salma agrees. He stands in the bathroom next to her, and they brush their teeth together. He grabs her a glass of water and her favorite fairy doll and pulls the sheets over her head, jokingly.

"Baba!" she shouts, and he pulls them back down, laughing.

Salma smiles and asks Baba if he is happy about his surprises today.

"Salma, you and Mama did a fantastic job," he says. "Honestly, this place feels like home."

Salma nods. She, too, feels like she's at home. It feels as if both Damascus and Vancouver are here with them. That feels right to her: she doesn't feel the tears burning in her eyes. "It's like my heart is big enough to carry both Damascus and Vancouver," Salma says.

"You have the biggest heart in the whole universe, Salma," Baba says. He stands up, switches off the bedside light, and wishes Salma goodnight.

"Do you still miss Damascus, Baba?" Salma asks.

"Every day. I really do," Baba says.

"I miss it, too." Salma smiles. "But it's okay to have two homes at the same time, Baba," she says. "One right here," she says, gesturing at their Canadian home, "and one hiding right here." Salma points to her own chest, right where her heart beats. Baba smiles and kisses Salma's forehead before heading to the door.

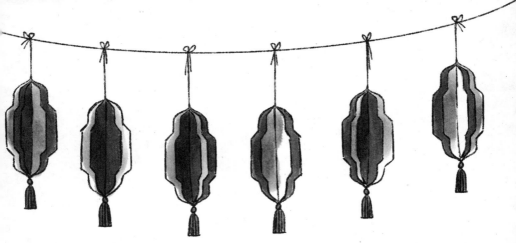

Build a lantern like Salma!

What you need:

- Four pieces of yarn in the color of your choice:
  - One piece about two feet long
  - Two short pieces about three inches long
  - One piece about one foot long (for securing onto the lantern at the end)
- A square piece of cardboard (about 3 inches by 3 inches)
- Scissors
- Two colorful sheets of paper
- Pencil
- Glue stick
- Lantern template on page 97

First, let's make the tassel:

1. Take your longest piece of yarn and hold one end against the side of the cardboard square.

2. Wrap the yarn around the cardboard. Keep going until you run out of yarn.

3. Take one of the short pieces of yarn, slide it between the wrapped yarn and the top of the cardboard, and then tie it into a tight double knot.

4. Slide the tassel off the cardboard.

5. Tie the other short piece of yarn about 1 inch from the top of the tassel (where you just tied the double knot) as tightly as you can. You can tie multiple knots to make sure it's secure.

6. Cut through the bottom loop of the tassel.

7. Take your remaining piece of yarn and tie it at the top of the tassel, so you can secure it to your lantern later. Your tassel is now done!

Second, let's make the lantern:

1. Cut out the template on page 97.

2. Trace the template four times on each of two colorful sheets of paper. You should have drawn eight lanterns.

3. Cut out all eight lantern pieces.

4. Fold each lantern piece in half, lengthwise (hot-dog style).

5. Take one folded lantern piece and put glue on one side. Take a second folded piece (in the other color) and put it on top of the piece you just glued. Then, glue on top of this second piece and attach a third piece (the first color). Keep gluing alternating colors of lantern pieces until you have a stack of all eight lantern pieces.

6. Add your tassel: Find the spot where the first and last lantern pieces meet and put some glue down the center. Take your tassel with the long yarn hanging from the top and secure the yarn in the center of the lantern, making sure the end of the yarn pokes out at the top of the lantern (for hanging) and your tassel is hanging down below the bottom of the lantern.

7. To secure your tassel, glue the side of the last lantern piece to the side of the first piece to close the lantern and hold the hanging yarn and tassel in place.

Your lantern is now complete!

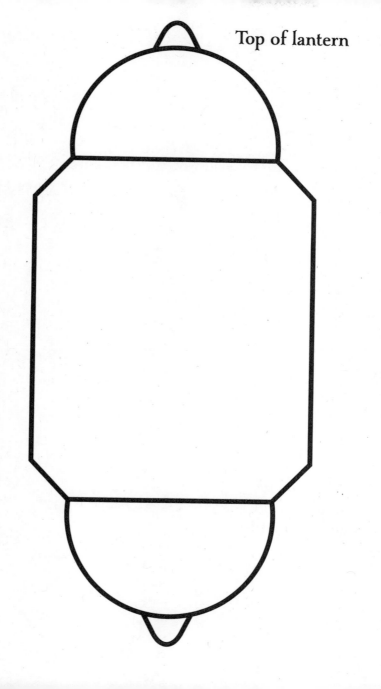

Top of lantern

Keep reading for a sneak peek of Book 2!

Chapter 1

Salma fills in the last bits of sky in her family portrait. The blue goes nicely with Vancouver's green forests stretching in the background; the Fraser River twirls throughout. The mountains, tall and capped with white snow, tower over the scene. She adds a beautiful mosaic border around her drawing, then decorates it with jasmine flowers and little birds. In the center, Salma draws her mama and baba holding hands. Salma adds herself beside Baba, with a big smile on her face.

Beside Mama, Salma draws her uncle, Khalou Dawood.

"Salma, can you go downstairs and help your baba?" Mama says from the kitchen. Salma leaves the coloring pencils scattered on her bed, takes a final look at her work, and rushes out of her room.

"I am really excited for my khalou's visit," she says as she pulls on her rain boots.

"Me, too!" Mama holds Salma's jacket open so Salma can get her arms into the sleeves. "I haven't seen my brother in so long!"

Salma slips into the hallway and runs to the elevator.

Salma has heard about her uncle, Khalou Dawood, for as long as she can remember. He left Syria and came to Canada years before she was born. He studied at a university in a faraway city called Toronto, then found a job and stayed. But Khalou Dawood moved to Vancouver recently, and now he's finally visiting them in their new home.

The elevator opens on the garage floor. Salma spots Baba pulling the last bag out of the trunk of their car. He hands it to Salma, and she is surprised it's not full of groceries like all the others. The cloth bag has Salma's favorite bookstore logo on it.

"Wow!" Salma says. "Did you buy me new coloring books?"

"No, Salma, these books are for your mother and I."

Salma sneaks a look at the titles. She can read them but isn't sure what they mean.

"Have you ever met my khalou, Baba?" Salma asks as they ride the elevator back to their floor.

"I did, once, a long time ago—way before you were born," Baba says.

Salma has never had an uncle before. Her friends tell her of the adventures their favorite uncles take them on, like a day trip to the amusement park, or a night drive to a kids' theatre show, and the many candies and toys they offer. Riya's uncle even lets her play her favorite songs loud in his car when he drives them somewhere. Now, Salma will get to do all of this, too. And it will be even more fun, because Khalou Dawood will be the best khalou in the whole wide world.

"Why hasn't he visited us before?" Salma asks. *Toronto might be far, but it's not as far as Syria. Ayman's khalou even visited once from Prince Edward Island,*

and that's so far away, the sun rises there four hours before it does in Vancouver.

"You will have to ask your Mama." The elevator doors open, and she follows him out.

Salma takes the books to her parents' bedroom. Then, she sets the table while Mama organizes ingredients next to a big cooking pot, preparing for the big meal.

"Why hasn't my khalou visited us before, Mama?" Salma asks, but Mama doesn't answer right away. Salma looks over and sees Mama standing still, holding the lid of the pot. Her eyes look faraway and her lips quiver.

"Mama?" Salma says.

Mama snaps out of her trance. She takes a deep breath, puts the lid down, then sprinkles some spices on the meal. But she still doesn't answer Salma. She is about to ask her question again when Mama finally looks her in the eyes.

"When we were young," Mama says, "your khalou and I used to play pranks on your grandparents all the time."

"Oh, so that's where Salma gets her pranks from!" Baba jokes from the couch.

"No. My pranks are all original," Salma teases. "No one is a better prankster than me!"

Everyone laughs. Salma smiles, too, proud of her joke. But Mama still has not answered her question. There is something her parents don't want to talk about. She knows it's not polite to insist, but curiosity is overwhelming her.

A few hours later, the smell of fried eggplants and minced meat fills the apartment.

"I'll get it!" Salma shouts when the doorbell rings. She swings open the door and finds her khalou on the other side. She recognizes him from photos: he is tall, with brown skin glimmering like sand on the riverbank, and wide black eyes. She jumps into his arms, and he gives her a big squeeze.

"Salma! What a big girl you are!"

"I am the tallest girl in my class!" she announces proudly.

"I am sure you are also the smartest." He pats her hair.

"Dawood!" Mama passes Salma and hugs her brother. She kisses him on both cheeks, then pulls him in for a second hug.

"It has been too long." Khalou shakes Baba's hand. The family gathers in the living room, and Salma sits right by her khalou's side. She listens as the family chitchats, laughs at her baba's jokes, and watches her mama dote on her brother.

"I wish I'd met you years ago, Khalou," Salma says, and Khalou pulls her in for a hug. Finally, Salma asks the question that's been on her mind. "Why haven't you come to visit before?"

The grown-ups go silent. Baba's face is concerned, and Mama's has the same look she had earlier: like she's remembering something sad. Khalou hesitates, then finally says, "You see, Salma, your mama and I had a big fight."

"We don't talk about this anymore," Mama interrupts. Her voice is a bit too loud.

"Salma is growing up in Canada, sister," Khalou insists. "I won't be the last man she meets who is married to another m—"

"No. Please stop talking." Mama interrupts again. This time, there is anger in her eyes, as if Khalou broke her favorite vase or spilled rice all over the living room floor.

Khalou takes a deep breath. He looks at Mama as if he is about to say something, then rests his eyes on Salma and gives her a small smile. "Yes, you are right," he says to Mama. "We won't talk about this."

"Let's eat, then," Mama says quickly.

At the dinner table, it's as if someone broke glass dishes all over the floor, and everyone is afraid to step on a sharp piece. Salma wiggles in her seat. She imagined her first meeting with Khalou to be filled with happy moments, but instead it's tense. What are the grown-ups not telling her?

About the Author

© Amanda Palmer

DANNY RAMADAN made Canada his home in 2014 after leaving his homeland of Syria and becoming a refugee in Lebanon. Since then, Danny has written multiple books for both kids and grown-ups. People seem to think Danny knows how to write well. To his surprise, they keep asking him for more books.

In Vancouver, the place Danny calls home, he met Matthew, the love of his life, and married him. The two adopted the bestest dog in the world, Freddie, who is named after a singer from the '80s you are too young to know and who exclusively naps in Danny's lap every afternoon. When Danny is not writing, he is playing video games.

About the Illustrator

Just like Salma, ANNA BRON moved to Canada with her family when she was very young. She remembers helping her parents with English and making friends in school with kids from all over the world. She always loved to draw from her imagination and when she grew up, she became an illustrator and animator. She gets to work on lots of fun projects, from drawing kids' books to designing unique characters and working on short animated films. Her favorite things to draw are horses, birds, and mountains. When she's not drawing, she loves getting outside to hike and ski.